MW01134242

Books by Paige Sleuth

Cozy Cat Caper Mystery Series:

HALLOWEEN *in* CHERRY HILLS

COZY CAT

A

CAPER

MYSTERY BOOK

7

PAIGE SLEUTH

Copyright © 2016 Marla Bradeen
(writing as Paige Sleuth)

All rights reserved.

ISBN: 1533392374
ISBN-13: 978-1533392374

Published by Marla Bradeen.

This book or portions of it (excluding brief quotations) may not be reproduced without prior written permission from the publisher/author.

This book is a work of fiction. Names, characters, businesses, places, events, and incidents are either products of the author's imagination or used in a fictitious manner. Any resemblance to actual persons (living or dead), actual businesses, or actual events is purely coincidental.

CHAPTER ONE

"Halloween is tomorrow," Katherine Harper said, reaching over to pet her cat Matilda. "That's less than eight hours away."

Matty's eyelids slipped shut, the room filling with the sound of her purring. The tortoiseshell was curled up in her favorite spot on the couch, her yellow-and-brown body compacted into a tight ball and her white chin facing outward in order to be easily accessible for scratching.

"So?" Andrew Milhone asked. Tom, Kat's other cat, was stretched out on his back along Andrew's legs, thrilled to be on the receiving end of a vigorous belly rub.

"So, I live in a secure apartment building," Kat replied.

Andrew grinned. "Then you'll be safe from the crazies."

Kat rolled her eyes. "My point is, nobody is going to come trick-or-treating here. We'll be bored out of our minds. It would be more fun to spend Halloween somewhere else, don't you think?"

Tom flipped over and rested his chin on his paws, a sure sign the brown-and-black cat had finally gotten enough attention—for now.

Andrew settled back against the couch. "In that case, I vote for Aruba. They don't celebrate Halloween there, do they? We can relax on the beach sipping piña coladas while everyone back here in Cherry Hills has to deal with kids on a sugar high."

Kat sat up, a flash of exasperation searing through her. "Andrew, I'm trying to have a serious conversation and you're making jokes."

He frowned, the twinkle in his eyes dimming. "Okay, well, where do you want to spend Halloween? Seattle's only a two-hour drive. We could see what's happening over there."

Kat rubbed Matty's ears. "I don't want to go to Seattle. I was thinking of something a little closer to home."

"You mean Wenatchee?"

"Closer. Like, your place."

Andrew's mouth dropped open. "My place?" The words emerged as a squeak.

"Yes." Kat stopped petting Matty so she could twist toward Andrew. "If you haven't noticed, I've never actually been inside your house."

He swallowed. "I realize that."

"We always hang out here." Kat looked around her apartment and grimaced. "This place is so small. Don't you get tired of it?"

"Not really."

"Well, I do. Besides, I want to see where you live."

Andrew stared at her. She stared back. She only looked away when Matty crawled into her lap and nudged her hand with her head. Clearly Matty hadn't appreciated being ignored while the humans were talking.

Kat stroked the tortoiseshell, but her mind was still on her conversation with Andrew. She couldn't see what the problem was. It wasn't as if she had proposed marriage. She just wanted to see his house.

The full force of her stubbornness kicked in then. She made a silent vow not to back down until he agreed.

Andrew shifted positions, creating enough of a disruption that Tom jumped onto the floor and stalked off. The sound of crunching kibble drifted out of the kitchen seconds later.

Andrew coughed. "You know, my place isn't really that interesting. It's old, and I'm not much of a decorator."

Kat held up her palms. "So?"

Matty reached up and swatted Kat's hand. Kat wasn't sure if the animal was taking Andrew's side or if she was simply miffed about being ignored again.

Andrew raked his fingers through his hair, sending a sandy lock flopping over his forehead. "The roof has a couple leaks. It's really annoying when you want some peace and quiet and all you can hear is a steady drip-drip-drip."

"Luckily, the forecast for tomorrow includes a zero percent chance of rain."

He crossed then uncrossed his ankles. "My neighbors can be kind of loud."

"Andrew!" Kat slapped her hands on the couch cushions, much to Matty's dismay. "I don't care! I don't care about your neighbors, or your lack of interior design skills, or a few leaks. I wouldn't even care if you had a bubbling brook running through your living room. I just want to see where you live. Is that so strange? I mean, we've been dating for a couple months now, and I've never been inside your house. That can't be normal."

His face paled, and she felt a ping of alarm.

"Is there a reason you don't want me to see your house?" she asked, her voice growing quieter. She was having trouble getting the words out around the lump developing in her throat. "Are you ashamed your neighbors will see me with you or something?"

"What?" He straightened. "No."

"Then what is it?"

"It's—I'm—" He huffed, then stood up to pace around the room.

Dread pooled in Kat's stomach. "Just tell me."

He must have heard the pleading note in her voice. He pivoted around to face her. "I'm nervous."

"Nervous?" She took a moment to absorb that. "Nervous about what? That I'm going to judge you?"

He stared at her for what felt like half an hour. The anguish written all over his face made Kat's chest tighten. When he finally did speak, his words tumbled out in a rush.

"I'm afraid I'll let you in, and then you'll leave."

"I won't leave, even if I hate the house. I promise. I'll even bring an umbrella, just in case it does rain."

He blew out a breath. "You're not getting it. I'm afraid you'll *leave* leave."

Understanding dawned. "You mean break up with you."

He dragged his hand down his face. "Yes."

The pressure in Kat's chest eased. Now that she knew what his problem was, it would be a cinch to banish his concerns. "Andrew, I'm with you for you, not your house."

He regarded her for a moment before saying, "Do you remember my uncle Don?"

Kat thought back to when she and Andrew had been kids in the Cherry Hills foster care system, but she couldn't recall ever meeting one of Andrew's uncles. "No."

"He lived in Spokane," Andrew said, his voice hollow. He turned to stare at something across the room. "We were in touch off and on back before you left town after high school."

Tom ambled out of the kitchen. He sat down near the edge of the living room, running his tongue over his lips as he always did after a satisfying meal.

"When I moved into my first solo apartment, no roommates, we happened to be in one of those periods where we were in touch. Uncle Don came over to visit. He brought beer—to celebrate, he said." Andrew paused, working his jaw. "I should have taken his keys right when he showed up at the door, but I was afraid to ask."

Kat stilled, her fingers freezing on Matty's back as a sick feeling developed in the pit of her stomach. She had a good idea what he was going to say before he voiced the words.

Andrew turned to stare out the window. "He crashed on his way home that night. He died upon impact."

Kat felt her heart snap in two. "You can't blame yourself for that."

Andrew looked at her over his shoulder. "What if I told you Uncle Don blames me?"

Matty lifted her head, her green eyes opened wide. Tom, who had been licking one paw, stopped moving altogether. Andrew's statement seemed to have shocked the felines as much as it had Kat.

Andrew took a deep breath. "I've dated a couple other girls over the years, and it seems whenever I invite them over, a week later we've broken up. It doesn't matter where I live. It happened in my old apartments, and it happened after I bought the house I live in now."

Kat's throat constricted. "I'm not those girls, Andrew."

"I know, but . . ." He lifted one shoulder. "I don't really believe in ghosts and I realize this sounds ridiculous, but I can't shake the sense that Uncle Don is still angry at me for letting him die, that he's punishing me by chasing away anybody who gets too close."

"You didn't *let* him die," Kat said. "He was an adult. He should have known better."

"We were both adults. I could have stopped him."

"Andrew." Kat started stroking Matty again, using the rhythmic motion to steady herself. "Your uncle alone is responsible for what happened to him. And those other girls, they were fools to break up with you."

Andrew's cheek twisted. "I knew you wouldn't get it. You're a skeptic, same as me—most of the time."

"Andrew," she began before the sound of her cell phone cut through the air. She raised her voice to be heard above it. "I wouldn't leave —"

"You should answer that," Andrew interrupted.

Kat flapped her hand. "Whoever it is can leave a voicemail."

"I need a drink." He spun on his heel and stalked past Tom into the kitchen.

Kat, Matty, and Tom all watched him. Kat fingered the edge of the couch, torn between going after him and giving him some space.

Matty settled the matter for her. She leapt onto the coffee table and used her nose to nudge the phone closer.

Kat sighed as she snatched it up. "Hello?"

"Kat," Imogene Little said, sounding almost breathless, "something urgent has come up."

CHAPTER TWO

"I'm so glad y'all are here," Tracy Montgomery said, one hand resting on her abdomen as she reclined against the couch.

Imogene patted Tracy's knee. "Helping animals in need is what our organization does."

Tracy gripped Imogene's hand like a lifeline. "I wasn't sure, since y'all are Furry Friends *Foster* Families. I thought maybe y'all just helped homeless animals, but Willow said I should call anyway."

Willow Wu wrung her hands together. "This is all my fault. I was supposed to be watching Midnight while you were out of town."

Kat crossed her legs, studying the trio from the armchair on the other side of Tracy's living room. Although all three women were petite, their physical similarities ended there.

On one end of the couch sat Imogene, the president of the Furry Friends Foster Families nonprofit organization. She was dressed as Kat was used to seeing her, in jeans and a simple T-shirt with her auburn hair pulled back in a ponytail. The fifty-something woman seemed to be the most put together emotionally, although Kat could tell from the way her foot twitched that Imogene was as worried as everyone else.

Willow occupied the other end of the sofa. Kat put the 4F secretary in her forties, but her Asian genes gave her the appearance of someone ten years younger. Right now Willow looked immaculate in a gray blouse and matching slacks. Worry lines framed her eyes and mouth, but that was the only indication of her distress. Her straight, jet-black hair looked to have been professionally styled, and her complexion was flawless.

Tracy sat between them. With her wrinkled blouse and uncombed blond hair, she appeared to have been interrupted in the middle of a nightmare. Kat pegged Tracy as close to her age of thirty-two, but the stress of her situation had aggravated the bags under her eyes, making her look twenty years older.

Sitting opposite the trio, Kat felt a little like the odd woman out. Tracy and Willow both taught at Cherry Hills High, and Imogene obviously knew Tracy from around town. That left Kat as the only 4F board member just now meeting the distressed math teacher.

But she wasn't here to make friends, Kat reminded herself. They were here to deal with Tracy's crisis.

Tracy pulled at a loose thread hanging from the bottom of her blouse. "He's pure black, you know, not a white patch on his body. An all-black cat out there by himself the day before Halloween . . ."

Imogene squeezed Tracy's leg. "Could he have snuck over to one of the neighbors'?"

Tracy shook her head. "He's afraid of the outdoors. He would never venture outside on his own." She broke off in a sob, burying her face in her hands.

Kat's stomach knotted in commiseration. If Matty or Tom ever went missing, she was pretty sure she would be falling apart too. The fact that Tracy had spent all morning and afternoon traveling from Memphis back to Cherry Hills couldn't be good for the state of her nerves either. Tracy's luggage was still piled in one corner of her living room, forgotten in the wake of the tragedy that had greeted her upon her return home.

Tracy swiped at the tears streaking down her cheeks. "Anybody could have grabbed him. I don't reckon he would have run. He's so friendly, and he's had only good experiences with people. He doesn't know how evil some folks can be."

Imogene shifted her attention to Willow. "When did you last see him?"

"Last night, when I performed my evening check on him," Willow said. "I fed him, cleaned out his box, and gave him some attention before I left. That would have been around seven. He was sitting right over there on his kitty perch when I let myself out the front door."

Kat glanced at the empty cat perch, a pinch in her chest.

"This morning when I stopped by before my first class and saw he wasn't here, I called Tracy right away," Willow went on. "I thought perhaps he had discovered a new spot, but when I searched the house he was nowhere to be found."

"And I checked every possible hidey-hole

the minute I got home," Tracy said. "But he's gone. Missing."

"You're sure he was here when you left last night?" Imogene asked Willow.

"Positive. And I *know* I didn't leave any windows open." Willow sat up straighter. "Somebody had to have broken in and taken him. It's the only explanation."

"I have that number lock on my door instead of a key lock," Tracy said. "Some hooligan could have figured out my code and used it to break in."

Imogene patted her shoulder. "We're going to do our best to find him."

"I'm so worried somebody bad took him." Tracy's lower lip quivered. "This time of year, you just don't know what people are thinking."

Willow bobbed her head. "Like that witch next door."

"Connie's not a witch," Tracy said. "She's just . . . eccentric."

Willow rubbed her hands up and down her arms. "Well, she gives me the heebie-jeebies."

"She claims she talks to ghosts," Tracy told Imogene. "That's how she earns her living. She has to behave a little kooky so people feel they got their money's worth and come back for more."

"Did Connie know you were going out of town?" Imogene asked.

"Yes, but everybody and their brother knew I was out of town. I've been so excited about becoming an auntie that my sister's baby shower is all I've talked about this past month." Tracy glanced at the clock on the wall and her face crumpled. "It's going on right now, you know. I hope they're managing okay without me."

"This isn't your fault," Willow said. "If anyone is to blame, it's me."

"You were doing me a favor." Tracy grabbed a tissue out of the box on the coffee table and blew her nose. "And you weren't the one who ran your mouth all over town about me going to Tennessee for a week."

Kat's gaze drifted around the room, her heart aching as she took in the toy mice, plastic balls, and plush beds scattered around. The abundance of cat items made Midnight's absence all the more palpable.

Imogene set her palm on Tracy's arm. "Do you have a picture of him?"

"I have thousands." Tracy fished a cell phone out of her pants pocket, punched a few buttons, and handed the phone to Imogene. "Here."

Kat stood up and moved closer to the couch, looking over Imogene's shoulder at the photo Tracy had pulled up. In it, a black cat sat on a spiral notebook, his tail tucked around his paws. His head was tilted slightly to the side, his yellow eyes bright and innocent as he peered at the camera.

Kat wrapped her arms around herself, a chill inching down her spine. For Midnight's sake, she hoped he hadn't fallen into the wrong hands.

Imogene clucked her tongue. "Oh, look at that face."

"He's even cuter in person." Tracy smiled for the first time since Kat had met her. "And he loves sitting on that grade book of mine, particularly when I'm trying to write in it. He's my big baby."

"He sounds just like a real baby too," Willow chimed in. "Every time I walked through that door he greeted me with a wail."

"He cries when he's hungry. Or scared." Tracy's smile faded as quickly as it had appeared, her gaze sliding toward the cell phone in Imogene's hands. "Oh, I reckon he's meowing up a storm right now."

"Then he'll be that much easier to find."
Imogene handed Tracy's cell back to her. "I
want you to call everyone you know who has
some free time this evening. We're going to
organize a search party."

Tracy took the phone. "All right. But I don't
reckon Midnight escaped on his own."

"Even if he was taken, there's a chance he
got away," Imogene said. "Since he's never been
outside, he could be across the street and not
know his own way home."

Willow pulled her own cell phone out of her
purse on the floor. "I'll call some of the other
teachers. They'll be happy to help."

"I'll join you guys tonight, after I get off
work," Kat said. She pointed to Tracy's phone.
"Email me that photo, and I'll get some fliers
made that we can post around town."

Tracy didn't appear to hear her, seemingly
lost in her own thoughts. When she swiveled
toward Imogene, Kat could see the raw fear
etched across her face. "Imogene, play it
straight with me now. Do you reckon he's gone
forever?"

Imogene looked her in the eye. "I promise
you, we are going to do our very best to find

him."

Kat leaned against the wall, her stomach tightening. She hadn't missed how Imogene's promise had failed to guarantee Midnight's safe return home.

CHAPTER THREE

It took Kat longer than she expected to create the fliers for Midnight. Someone more skilled probably could have accomplished the task in five minutes, but, although Kat was quite comfortable with computers, she wasn't the best graphic designer. It didn't help that Matty insisted on 'assisting' by sitting on the computer keyboard and batting at Kat's hand whenever she moved the mouse.

By the time she finally had a decent one-page layout, it was only twenty minutes before her waitressing shift at Jessie's Diner was due to start. She hoped getting the fliers printed wouldn't take long. Not only would the copy shop be closed by the time she got off work, but she hated to wait any longer than necessary to start circulating the fliers. Every passing second was one more second in which Midnight's situation could worsen.

Fortunately, there wasn't a line at the register when she arrived at the shop. She walked up to the lone girl manning the counter.

"Hi," Kat greeted. "I have some fliers I need printed out in bulk."

The girl smiled from behind her computer. Her name tag identified her as Lindsay. "Sure. Do you have one with you?"

Kat held up the memory stick she'd brought. "The file is saved on here."

Lindsay brushed a long, honey-blond lock of hair away from her face before taking hold of the memory stick. She popped it into one of the computer's USB ports and clicked around for a minute before her hand stopped moving.

"What is this?" Lindsay asked.

"Fliers for a missing cat. Somebody broke into his owner's house and took him."

Lindsay's blue eyes widened. "Somebody stole Ms. Montgomery's cat?"

"You know Tracy Montgomery?"

"She teaches at my school."

Kat processed that. Could one of Tracy's

students have taken Midnight? Tracy had said she'd told everyone about going to Tennessee. And even if she hadn't made an announcement to her students, the presence of a substitute teacher would have clued them in. One of them could have decided to get into some mischief while she was away. Perhaps they had filched Midnight as revenge for a bad grade or grueling assignment.

"Do you think somebody at Cherry Hills High might have taken Midnight?" Kat asked Lindsay.

Lindsay frowned as she fingered the mouse. "I guess it's possible, but why?"

"To punish her maybe. Do any of your classmates dislike her?"

Lindsay shook her head. "She tends to assign too much homework, but Ms. Montgomery is likable enough. She seems to really care about us."

The door chimed. A tall, lanky teenage boy walked in.

He eyed Lindsay, a grimace distorting his aquiline nose and thin lips. "You're not off yet?"

"I told you, we close at six," she replied.

He looked at the clock. "Can't you close up a few minutes early?"

"I'm with a customer, Luke." Lindsay turned toward Kat. "How many copies of these fliers did you want?"

"Fifty to start," Kat said.

Lindsay clicked a few times before the printer behind her started humming. After a second, it began spitting out pages.

The boy shoved his hands in his pockets and slouched against the wall. "I can't wait until you get your own car."

"Me neither." Lindsay started to roll her eyes but stopped herself, flushing when she caught Kat watching her. "This is my big brother, Luke," she said, gesturing toward the boy.

Kat smiled. "Hi."

He bobbed his head. "Yo."

"Luke, take a look at this." Lindsay picked up one of the pages collecting in the printer tray, holding it out to her brother.

Luke pushed away from the wall and loped over to the counter in two long strides.

Lindsay set the page on the counter. "This is Ms. Montgomery's cat. Do you know anything about him being missing?"

"No way." Luke jerked backward, clearly startled by his sister's accusation.

His defensiveness surprised Kat, prompting her to study him more closely. He towered over her five-foot-six-inch frame, but he was slender to the point of almost looking emaciated. He stayed slouched forward, his hands jammed into his jeans pockets. The way his eyes skirted around the store certainly made him look guilty of something.

Kat coughed, and Luke practically jumped out of his skin. He started speaking before Kat could.

"I've gotta split," he said, ostensibly to Lindsay although his eyes were fixed on the door. "Be back in a few."

Kat was tempted to chase after him as he raced out of the store, but he moved with a surprising speed. She watched him climb into a blue Honda parked outside and take off down the street.

"I wonder what the big rush is," Kat mumbled to herself.

She hadn't realized Lindsay had heard her until she said, "Who knows? He's been acting weird ever since his senior year started."

"Weird how?" Kat asked.

"Like, moody."

Kat waited for her to elaborate, but after

another moment she realized Lindsay would need some encouragement. "What do you think he's so moody about?"

"I'm guessing he's worried about what he's going to do after graduation," Lindsay said. "All his friends are talking about applying to college, something Luke has never been all that interested in. But now that he's almost done with high school, the pressure seems to be getting to him. I think he's starting to regret not taking school more seriously."

Kat nodded. "That makes sense."

Lindsay moved closer to the copier. "But anyway, that's not your problem."

"It is if he took Midnight," Kat replied, wondering if the stress of an unknown future might have spurred Luke to act out.

Lindsay grabbed some of the fliers. "He wouldn't have taken Midnight. I don't even know why I accused him. He's more the type to toilet-paper Ms. Montgomery's house if he had a problem with her."

Kat considered that. Tracy had claimed the house was exactly as she'd left it, which meant if Luke had gone over intending to trash the place something had made him abandon his plans. Could that something be Midnight? Maybe

Luke's presence or actions had frightened the cat, causing him to bolt outside. Except if he had left of his own volition, wouldn't he have returned home by now?

Maybe not, Kat conceded, if someone had snatched him before he could find his way back to the house.

She shivered. If that were the case, Midnight could be anywhere.

"Here are your fliers," Lindsay said, pushing the stack across the counter.

Kat took one off the top and handed it to Lindsay. "You can keep this one. If you hear something or get any ideas as to who might have taken Midnight, Tracy's number is listed there."

Lindsay took it. "I'll post this on the front door. Maybe one of our customers will have seen him."

"That would be great."

Kat settled the bill then grabbed the stack of fliers. She looked around as she exited the shop but didn't see the blue Honda anywhere. And as much as she wanted to stay and wait for Luke's return appearance, she was scheduled to be at work in five minutes.

CHAPTER FOUR

Jessie's Diner smelled delicious when Kat walked in. Her mouth immediately started watering, making her fully aware that she hadn't had time to eat since lunch.

"Whatever's on special, I'm going to be craving it my whole shift," Kat told Jessie Polanski as she stepped behind the counter.

"That would be the ravioli with pumpkin sauce," Jessie said, punching something into the cash register. "A fresh pot of sauce is simmering as we speak."

"If it tastes anything like it smells, it's going to be sold out before we close for the night."

"Based on how the pumpkin pancakes flew off the grill this morning, people can't get enough pumpkin this time of year. I'll save you a helping."

Kat grinned. "I knew I worked for you for a reason."

"You mean the fact that you haven't found a job in computers yet?"

"Something like that." Kat stuffed her purse under the counter and held up a few of the fliers she'd had printed out. "Do you mind if I tape these in the windows?"

"What are they?" Jessie asked.

"Lost cat fliers. Do you know Tracy Montgomery?"

"Yeah, sure."

Using her free hand, Kat grabbed an apron from a shelf under the counter and slipped it over her head. "Somebody broke into her house while she was out of town and took her cat Midnight."

Jessie grimaced. "That's awful."

"I know." The knot that had been present in Kat's stomach ever since she'd received Imogene's call grew larger. "She's especially worried with Halloween coming up."

"Ugh." Jessie pivoted around and rummaged through a basket next to the register. When she faced Kat again, she had a roll of tape in her hand. "Here. Post those wherever you want."

Kat took the tape and headed toward the front of the restaurant. She had finished affixing fliers to most of the windows when a man, woman, and teenage girl approached.

Kat held the door open for them. "Good evening. Welcome to Jessie's."

The woman, a middle-aged brunette, smiled at Kat as she stepped inside. "Thank you."

The man grinned wide enough to expose his molars. "We heard you've got pumpkin pancakes on special."

"We did," Kat said, smiling back at him, "for breakfast."

"I'll whip you up a plate, Trevor," Jessie called from behind the counter. "Complete with maple butter and slivered pecans."

"Thanks, Jess." The man flopped into the closest booth. "You certainly know the way to a man's heart."

The woman plucked a menu from behind the napkin dispenser as she slid next to him. "They have good salads here. You should try one."

Trevor made a face. "Salads are for rabbits."

The girl followed at a distance, not saying

anything as she slumped into the seat across from the two adults.

Kat stepped up to the table. "Can I get you something to drink?"

"A vanilla milkshake for me," Trevor said. "And you might as well tell Jessie to start cooking me those pancakes. I'm starving."

"Trevor, do you really think that's the healthiest thing you can order?" the woman asked. "You heard what your doctor said during your last checkup. You're supposed to be watching your cholesterol."

Trevor tapped her on the nose. "It's the holidays, m'dear Monica. Cholesterol concerns go out the window this time of year, not to appear again until New Year's."

Monica pursed her lips. "It's not the holidays yet. Thanksgiving is another month away."

"I'm talking about Halloween, my favorite holiday of the year."

Monica groaned. "Halloween is not a proper holiday."

"It is so. Just ask Beth."

The girl rolled her eyes, not saying anything.

"C'mon, don't be like that," Trevor said, a pleading note creeping into his voice. "You love Halloween as much as I do."

"I hate Halloween." Beth slunk toward the window lining one end of the booth seat, as if she wished it would swallow her up.

Trevor reached out and patted Beth's shoulder. "You say that now because things have been so difficult recently. But you'll regain your love of Halloween. I guarantee it."

"And Mom's right," Beth went on, ignoring his speech. "Halloween isn't a real holiday. If it was, we'd get the day off from school."

"You do have the day off," Trevor replied. "Tomorrow's Saturday."

Beth tilted her chin up. "Then they would have given us today off."

Kat cleared her throat, feeling like an intruder eavesdropping on a private family matter. "So, one vanilla milkshake. What other beverages should I bring?"

Nobody appeared to hear her. Instead, Monica now had her attention focused on the window.

"Hey, Beth," she said, pointing to one of the fliers Kat had taped to the glass minutes ago, "isn't Tracy Montgomery your math teacher?"

Beth's gaze flitted toward the flier before drifting away. "Yeah."

"And she's missing her cat?" Monica clucked

her tongue. "How awful."

"He's probably just hiding under a bed," Trevor said. "That's how cats are."

Monica squinted at him. "How do you know how cats are? You're allergic."

"That doesn't mean I'm not savvy on their ways." He winked at Kat. "You don't have to have a cat to know they can't resist a good nook or cranny. I've seen it on YouTube. They're always getting themselves into the most bizarre places."

"That's true," Kat conceded. "But in this case Midnight really is missing. Tracy was out of town when somebody broke in and took him."

Monica lifted one hand to her heart. "Somebody broke into her house?"

Kat nodded. "She has a keyless entry system, where you punch in a number to unlock the door. Somebody must have figured out her code."

"We have one of those too," Monica said, raising her eyebrows. She looked at Trevor. "I've been telling you we need to change the entry code every couple of months."

"It's on my to-do list," he replied.

"You keep adding to that list, but nothing

ever seems to get done," Monica said, but she sounded more amused than annoyed.

Trevor wagged his index finger back and forth. "Not true. I took Beth shopping for Halloween supplies just this afternoon."

"I told you you didn't have to." A shadow crossed over Beth's face. "And you didn't have to show up after school like that either. I know my way home, you know. I'm not a baby."

"Well, if I didn't take you Halloween shopping, those kids would be awfully disappointed tomorrow," Trevor said.

"Who cares about them?" Beth retorted. "Besides, I'll be in Wenatchee tomorrow."

"Wenatchee?" Monica glanced at Trevor.

He shrugged. "I guess we're taking a trip to see Nana."

"Not we, me." Beth folded her arms over her chest. "Luke's driving me."

Monica whipped toward her. "Luke?"

Beth glared at her. "Don't start. I love him."

Kat raised her eyebrows, wondering if Beth's Luke was the same Luke she'd met at the copy shop. Kat had to admit that, visually at least, they made a good pair. Beth was on the tall and slim side too, although, like Luke, her posture could use some work.

But Monica evidently didn't believe the couple was as well matched as Kat did. Although she refrained from saying anything, Kat could tell from the way her lips had puckered that she didn't approve of her daughter's beau.

Trevor snapped his fingers. "We'll take you to see Nana. We miss her too."

Beth's eyes were hard as she looked at him. "You're the ones who put her in the home."

The light in Trevor's eyes went out. "She's sick, honey. With her mind deteriorating the way it is, she can't be trusted to live by herself any longer."

Beth didn't respond. Instead, she kept her gaze trained out the window, a scowl on her face.

Monica sighed. "Poor Mom. I don't think she understands why we had to move her out of her apartment."

Trevor rubbed her shoulder. "Ah, she'll get used to it. This is a transitional period for her." He looked at Beth. "For all of us."

Beth wheeled around to glower at him. If her eyes were lasers, Trevor would have twin holes seared straight through his chest.

Kat jerked her thumb behind her. "Why don't I get you all waters to start." She was growing increasingly uncomfortable with the direction of this conversation and felt she should give the family some privacy.

Monica looked up, her eyes widening a fraction as if she were startled to note that Kat was still present. "Water would be wonderful. Thank you."

Trevor patted his stomach. "Bring me an order of those pancakes too."

Monica frowned, her gaze landing on Trevor's belly. "Actually, don't put in any orders yet. Please give us a moment to decide first."

Kat nodded, backing away as Trevor's shoulders sagged. She had a sneaking suspicion that by the time she returned with their waters, Trevor would have opted to order a salad instead.

CHAPTER FIVE

" You really can't do anything to help find Midnight?" Kat asked, glancing at Andrew.

He looked pointedly around them. "I'm out here looking for him, aren't I?"

The night was cool. Kat had on a heavy orange sweater, not so much in honor of Halloween but to minimize the risk of a car hitting her on this residential street. The moon and houses provided some light, but Kat wasn't taking any chances.

She tightened her hold on Matty's leash as the feline sniffed at a crack in the sidewalk. "I meant, couldn't you help in a professional capacity?" she asked. "As a police detective, you should have the power to open a new case or something."

"Like I said, I can get one of my colleagues to file a report if Tracy wants to go down to the station and give them a statement, but there's no evidence of a crime." Andrew shone his flashlight at a row of hedges lining the sidewalk. "Even Tracy claims nothing was stolen."

"You mean except Midnight."

"A missing cat isn't enough grounds for the police to open an investigation."

Matty grew bored with this section of sidewalk and trotted farther ahead. Kat followed behind her.

Andrew walked beside Kat. "I still don't understand why you brought Matty."

"If Midnight's been out here, she might be able to sniff out where he went," Kat said. "Plus, she has excellent night vision."

"She's a cat," Andrew replied. "She has no idea what we're doing out here."

"Tracy let her smell Midnight's favorite toy so she would be sensitive to his scent, remember?"

"She's not a bloodhound, Kat." Andrew watched Matty as she pounced on a leaf lying in the grass. "If anything, that toy mouse led her to believe we're out here hunting for rodents—or catnip. That thing reeked of the stuff."

Kat shrugged. "Well, she wanted to come."

"She's a cat," Andrew said again, as if that response was the only answer needed where Matty was concerned.

"Tom didn't want to come," Kat pointed out.

"Yeah, because he hates wearing a harness."

Kat knew he was right, not only about Tom but about the odds of Matty locating Midnight. Still, the cat's chances couldn't be any worse than hers.

Andrew aimed his flashlight down the street. "If you want my opinion, all this is a waste of time. You of all people know how sneaky cats can be. I bet Midnight slipped past Willow without her realizing it, and he comes strolling home whenever he feels like it."

"Even if he did take off voluntarily, that doesn't change the fact that he's in danger of being found by the wrong person the longer he's away from home."

A bleakness settled over Kat. She had never noticed before how many places there were for a cat to hide outside. And a black cat out at this time of night would be almost impossible to see. He'd blend right in with the shadows.

They walked for several yards without speaking. Only Matty seemed to be fully enjoying the outing. Her green eyes were wide, drinking in their surroundings. She wanted to sniff everything, her tail wagging every now and then when she caught a whiff of something particularly interesting.

Kat found herself holding her breath whenever Matty paused to take a closer look at a leaf or a pebble or a blade of grass. Had Midnight touched one of those things? Was this the path his abductors had taken while ferreting him away?

Kat kept her own eyes out for Midnight as she let Matty lead her. Her heart stopped when her flashlight caught on a scarecrow positioned in someone's front yard. With its beady black eyes and extended straw arms, it looked as if it were lunging at them.

She took a deep breath. Not only did being around all these Halloween decorations after dark spook her more than she had expected, but they also reminded her of the urgency of Midnight's situation.

Please be safe, she thought.

Andrew pointed his flashlight at a cluster of jack-o'-lanterns in someone's driveway. "I've gotta say, eleven o'clock at night doesn't strike me as the best time to go hunting for a black cat."

"I promised I'd help after work," Kat said. "Besides, I wouldn't be able to sleep knowing I didn't do anything to try to find him. I'm really worried about him."

"I understand." Andrew stopped walking. "We've reached the end of the block. You want to keep going or turn around?"

"Let's cross the street and head back," Kat suggested.

Andrew nodded, leading the way.

Somehow, everything looked different from the opposite side of the road. Kat's chest constricted as she once again took in all the places where Midnight could be hiding—and that was only counting the spots she could see. If Midnight had been taken somewhere, he could be miles away by now.

Matty veered toward the road, her leash pulling on Kat's fingers. She kept her head pointed forward, her eyes locked on to something in the distance.

Kat's heart rate sped up. "I think Matty sees something."

After checking for cars, she led Matty across

the street. She kept her flashlight pointed in front of them, hoping the beam reflected off of Midnight's eyes if he was the thing that had caught the tortoiseshell's interest.

Safely on the sidewalk again, Matty jogged purposefully forward before swerving into the yard of the house next to Tracy's. She stood there for a second, then she rotated her head toward Kat and meowed.

Kat crouched down and scratched Matty's back. "What do you see?"

Matty walked another yard before meowing again.

Kat stood back up and took a step forward.

"What are you doing?" Andrew asked, coming up behind them. "That's private property."

"Matty sees something over there."

"It's probably a squirrel."

Kat kept pace with the feline, who had started moving again. "You don't have to come if you're worried about trespassing."

Andrew didn't reply, but when she heard grass crunching behind her she knew he was following them. She was glad for that. She felt safer when he was around.

Matty slowed down, moving more cautiously now. She halted by a small sign sticking out of the grass, pausing to rub against it.

Kat aimed her flashlight at the sign, illuminating the words 'Spiritual Guidance Available Here—9 A.M. to 4 P.M. Mon-Sat or By Appointment.' Fake cobwebs hung from the edges of the sign—a tribute to Halloween, Kat supposed. At least, she hoped the cobwebs were only there for Halloween.

"Willow called the woman who lives here a witch," she whispered to Andrew, jerking her elbow toward the house.

"You know how people are. They love to sensationalize things."

Kat wondered briefly if he was referring to her and her concerns about Midnight. "Do you know her?"

Andrew snorted. "I would be the last person in Cherry Hills to associate with a so-called witch." He squinted at her. "Except maybe for you."

Kat couldn't argue with him there. They were both fairly skeptical of the supernatural—at least, she had always assumed so before he'd told her that story about his uncle. "But you might know her from around town," she said. "Her name is Connie. I don't know her last name."

"Doesn't sound familiar."

Kat stared at Connie's house. "I should knock on the door and ask if she's seen Midnight."

Andrew turned off his flashlight and tucked it into his jacket pocket. "You mean you want to snoop inside her house in case she took him."

"Well, Matty led us here for a reason."

"A neighborhood dog probably marked his territory on that sign. Matty likely just picked up on his scent."

Kat was ready to concede his point when her flashlight beam caught on something white near the base of the sign. She bent down to get a better look at the object, which turned out to be a small scrap of paper. She picked it up and held it in front of the flashlight. A series of six handwritten numbers was scrawled on the scrap.

Andrew poked his nose over her shoulder. "What's that?"

She showed him. "If I had to guess, this is the code to unlock Tracy's front door." She looked at Tracy's house. "Should we go ask her?"

"Her lights are off. After the day she's had, she has to be exhausted." Andrew extracted his cell phone and the flier Kat had given him with

Tracy's number on it. "I'll send her a text."

Kat's gaze drifted back toward Connie's house. "Do you think she has Midnight in there?"

"Not necessarily. Assuming you're right about somebody breaking into Tracy's house, they could have dropped this paper during their getaway. Connie's yard could have been their escape path."

Kat shivered despite the sweater. "What if Connie really is a witch?"

Andrew's thumbs stilled over the phone. "Don't tell me you believe in that stuff."

"You're the one who believes in ghosts."

Even in the dim light, she could see Andrew's jaw tense. "I don't really believe in ghosts," he said. "I've merely detected a pattern over the years and would be a fool to ignore it."

Kat sighed. "I guess it doesn't really matter what *we* believe anyway. If Connie thinks she can cast spells or whatever it is that witches do with black cats, that might have been enough of a reason for her to take Midnight."

"You have a point there."

Kat held Matty's leash a little tighter. "If she did grab him, what do you think she plans to do?"

"No clue." Andrew eyed the house. "But if you want my honest opinion, it wouldn't be good."

A cold breeze nipped at the exposed skin on Kat's face and hands. She had the same feeling.

CHAPTER SIX

Kat couldn't sleep that night. At Andrew's insistence, she had finally given up on searching for Midnight around one A.M. Tracy's text confirming that the code they'd found was for her front door only exacerbated Kat's worries about the missing feline.

While she tossed and turned, she made up her mind to pay a visit to Connie in the morning. If the witch had taken Midnight, perhaps Kat could find proof of her guilt inside her house. She figured the worst that could happen was she would be out whatever the going rate was for witch services.

Kat parked by the curb in front of Connie's house two minutes after nine. The place didn't seem as ominous in the light of day. The sign that had struck her as so creepy the night before now looked rather tiny and pathetic. The morning sun exposed it for what it really was, a raggedy bit of plywood that someone had stenciled letters on and hammered into the ground. The cobwebs were mere wisps of cotton.

Kat smoothed out her jacket as she headed up the driveway. A sign on the front door said 'Ring for Entry.' Steeling herself, she depressed the doorbell.

It didn't take long for the door to open. "Welcome to Casa de Vood," the raven-haired woman who answered said, waving Kat inside. "I am Madame Vood, and I will be helping you make a spiritual connection today."

"Oh." Kat stood rooted on the porch. "I was told a witch—er, fortune teller named Connie lived here."

Madame Vood bobbed her head. "Yes, yes, in this world I go by Constance. But I am not a witch, and I do not do fortunes. My specialty is eliminating the communication barriers present between those who exist in this world and those who inhabit alternate realities."

"Huh?" Kat had no idea what she was talking about.

"I am a spiritual guidance counselor," Madame Vood said. "I pass on messages from those who are not of this world."

"You mean ghosts," Kat said.

"Yes, yes. Also spirit guides, angels, loved ones that have passed on—whoever you wish to hear from."

Kat studied Madame Vood, starting to get the idea. If it could earn her a quick buck, she was willing to pretend to talk to anyone you wanted.

"Who have you come here to speak with?" Madame Vood asked.

Kat thought the answer was obvious. "You."

"Yes, yes. I am speaking of those not of our world."

"Oh. A ghost then, I guess."

Madame Vood peered at Kat. "You are searching for guidance, yes?"

"Sure." *Why not?* Kat figured.

"Then you are not interested in what a ghost has to say. Ghosts, they are rather self-centered. They are only here because of unfinished business, and that is all they want to discuss. Spirit guides and angels, they are more helpful."

Kat shrugged. "I'll talk to one of them then."

Movement inside the house caught her eye.

When she spotted a black cat strolling through Madame Vood's living room, her heart nearly burst out of her chest.

Madame Vood must have noticed Kat's reaction. She glanced behind her. "That is Sheba."

The cat evidently recognized her name. She stopped walking and twisted her head toward them, providing Kat with a clear view of the white patch gracing one side of her face. This cat was not Midnight.

Madame Vood tapped her chin with one finger. "You have a spiritual connection with animals, no?"

Kat took a deep breath, willing her heart rate to return to a more normal level. "I wouldn't go that far."

"Yes, you do." Madame Vood's tone brooked no room for argument. She flipped the sign on the door around so it read 'Session in Progress —Do Not Disturb' and waved Kat inside. "Come, I will summon your guides for you."

Kat scrutinized Madame Vood as she stepped over the threshold. Although she didn't know how spiritual guidance counselors normally dressed, Madame Vood's loose-fitting blue pants and flowing green-and-pink tunic looked appropriate. Her long, black hair zig-zagged around her face, giving her a somewhat wild look. Kat wouldn't be surprised to learn she'd stuck her finger in an electric socket after waking up this morning.

Kat shifted her focus to her surroundings. The house was dark, lit only by a dozen or so candles positioned around the living room. The heavy drapes blocked out any outside light. Rather than couches and a television, a tiny, round table occupied the center of the room. That and the three wooden chairs circling the table were the only pieces of furniture present, unless Kat counted the statues and weird abstract paintings lining the walls.

Kat's gaze landed on Sheba, who hadn't moved from her position on the floor. Judging by the reproachful look on her face and the way she was flicking her tail, Sheba was fully aware that Kat wasn't here for a spiritual session but rather to get her human in trouble.

Kat was somewhat disappointed that she hadn't seen any other cats hiding in the shadows. Of course, that didn't mean Madame Vood was innocent in Midnight's catnapping. She could be keeping the poor animal in a cage somewhere, waiting until nightfall before using him in some bizarre Halloween ritual.

The thought made Kat shiver.

"You find this world to be cold," Madame Vood said.

Kat spun around. "Excuse me?"

Madame Vood took a seat at the table, her movements displacing the candlelight and casting eerie shadows around the room. "You believe this world is a bad place."

Kat frowned. "I didn't say that."

"You did not have to say it with words. Your body speaks volumes."

Kat felt her defenses rising. She had to remind herself this was all an act.

"It is okay," Madame Vood said. "You keep your coat on. It will not interfere with my abilities." She extended her arms across the table. "Now give me your hand."

Kat didn't move. "Why?"

"So I can absorb your energy." Madame Vood's tone made it clear she felt she was stating the obvious.

"I thought you were just going to talk to my spiritual guides or something." The idea of a stranger pawing at her hand didn't sit well with Kat.

Madame Vood bobbed her head. "Yes, yes. I

will summon your guides. But hand first. I must form a bridge to your spirits."

Kat's eyes met Sheba's. Although the notion was ridiculous, she had the sensation that the feline was urging her to sit down.

Without warning, Madame Vood sprang out of her seat and grabbed Kat's right hand. Kat drew in a sharp breath. Her instinct was to pull back, but she stopped herself. After all, she was here under the pretense of wanting to benefit from Madame Vood's powers.

Madame Vood tugged Kat toward the table. "You sit."

Feeling trapped, Kat obeyed, although she stayed perched on the edge of the seat.

Madame Vood didn't let go of Kat's hand as she sat back down in her own chair. She hunched forward and traced the lines on Kat's palm with one finger. Her touch was light and cool, making Kat's skin tingle.

She lifted her head. "You are about to come into some money, in exactly three days."

"I thought you didn't tell fortunes," Kat said.

"I do not, but your palm does not lie." Madame Vood brought Kat's hand up to her nose and inhaled deeply. "Your skin smells like vast combination of foods. You work at Jessie's

Diner, yes? Same as one of my regulars. She always comes here after cashing paycheck, always on Tuesday."

Kat gawked at her, at a loss for words.

Madame Vood straightened, her eyes snapping shut. "I am getting a message."

"A message?"

"A spirit has presented himself to me. He wants you to know you are about to enter into a new world."

"A new world?" Kat repeated.

"Yes. A world fraught with resistance, but also where pieces come together to heal."

Kat frowned. She had no idea what that meant. It sounded like mumbo jumbo.

Sheba jumped into Kat's lap. Kat took the opportunity to pull her hand away, pretending she'd only done so to stroke the cat.

Madame Vood's eyes opened. "You and Sheba, you exist on the same spiritual plane," she said, sitting back in her chair while a slight smile played on her lips.

Kat figured that was just more mumbo jumbo. "Tell me, Con—Ms. Vood, do you have other cats besides Sheba?"

"The spirit says he is working to clear all obstacles from your path to this new world."

Kat blinked, wondering if Madame Vood had even heard her question.

"The spirit tells me he will send you a sign when you are safe to inhabit this new world," Madame Vood went on.

"What kind of sign?"

Madame Vood squeezed her eyes shut. "He is sending me a vision."

"A vision?"

"He is showing me a short, disfigured man in a cloak."

"Really?" Kat had to stifle a laugh. "What kind of people do these spirit guides associate with?"

"Spirit," Madame Vood corrected, her eyes opening. "This is not a spirit guide, just spirit."

"Oh. What's the difference?"

"This spirit is more like a guardian angel."

"O—kay," Kat said, drawing out the word.

Madame Vood held up a finger. "But he is not *your* guardian angel."

"What's he doing here then?" Kat asked. "Just hanging around?"

Madame Vood shook her head. "He does not hang. He is not confined by our physical limitations."

Kat didn't reply. She felt as if her head was

about to start spinning.

Madame Vood squinted at her. "You are having man troubles, no?"

Kat drew back a little. "What?"

"There is a man in your life."

"Yes," Kat admitted.

"He is holding back."

Kat lifted one shoulder, pushing away the memory of Andrew's protests about her visiting his house. "I wouldn't say that," she hedged.

"Yes, it is the truth." Madame Vood nodded once as though to indicate the topic was settled.

Kat felt a flash of irritation. "He's not. He's just . . . cautious, is all. His childhood wasn't easy."

"Yes, yes. No childhood is easy."

Kat rubbed Sheba's chin. "Well, Andrew's was particularly difficult."

Madame Vood tilted her head. "You are making excuses for him, no? The spirit says he is master of excuses. He tells me this man—Andrew, you call him—is not connected to his own mind. His intellect exists on a different plane than his soul."

Kat crooked one eyebrow. The way Madame Vood was speaking in tongues, Kat was having a hard time believing anyone could find this sort of session useful.

Madame Vood sat up suddenly and clapped her hands, causing Kat to flinch. "The spirit, he says he has no more to tell you. Now it is your turn. Reveal to me whom you wish to invoke."

Kat lifted Sheba off her lap and stood up. "Actually, I think I'm done." She set the cat on the floor and headed for the exit.

"Ah, but you have not yet found what you came here for."

Kat froze halfway to the door, thinking of Midnight. Madame Vood was right. She hadn't found what she had come here for.

Madame Vood pushed Kat's abandoned chair out using her foot. "You come, sit. We will summon spirit to guide you in the right direction."

The memory of Tracy bawling in her living room flashed through Kat's head. As much as she itched to get out of here, could she really walk away if there was even a sliver of a chance that Madame Vood might be able to tell her something that could lead them to the missing cat? Would she turn her back on a potential lead, however slim, if it were Matty or Tom missing instead of Midnight?

Kat stomped back over to the table and sank

into the chair. "Okay. What can you tell me?"

Madame Vood reached toward her. "You must give me your hand."

Kat folded her arms across her chest. "I did that earlier."

"Yes, yes. Now you must do so again."

Kat huffed, but she dutifully held out her hand.

Madame Vood took it. She closed her eyes again and tilted her face toward the ceiling. "I am getting a message from an angel," she said after a moment. "He tells me you are searching for a man."

Kat rolled her eyes, safe that Madame Vood couldn't see her. "I already have a man. Andrew, remember?"

"Different man," Madame Vood said. "A black man, no?"

Kat's mouth slipped open a little. Madame Vood couldn't possibly be talking about Midnight, could she?

"He is lost," Madame Vood continued. "You hope to guide him home."

Kat hunched closer, her heart skipping a beat. "Do you know where he is?"

"He is close."

"How close? Is he still in this neighborhood?"

Madame Vood opened her eyes and shook her head. "No, you do not understand. Angels, they do not measure distance like we do."

Kat frowned. "Can you at least tell me if he's still in Cherry Hills?"

"No, I cannot tell you anything. Only angel can say."

Kat blinked. "Well, why don't you ask him?"

Madame Vood ignored her. "The angel says you are not looking in the right place."

"Where is the right place?"

"I cannot tell you that," Madame Vood said, letting go of Kat's hand.

Kat scrunched up her nose. "Why not?"

"The angel will not reveal that information to me."

Kat swayed against the chair, figuring that was a good way for Madame Vood to absolve herself from any responsibility.

"But the angel says you cannot find him on your own," Madame Vood added. "You must invoke help."

Kat held up her hands. "Isn't that what I'm doing here?"

"Not my help."

"Whose then?"

"The angel will not share that with me."

Kat tried not to feel too disappointed. After all, this angel likely didn't even exist outside of Madame Vood's imagination. It was probably something she'd conjured up to wheedle a couple extra dollars out of Kat's wallet.

Madame Vood smiled and stood up. "You have gotten what you came here for, yes?"

Kat rose from her chair. "Not really."

"Yes, yes, you have." Madame Vood rubbed her palms together. "Now we must settle your bill, yes?"

CHAPTER SEVEN

Kat's mind was whirling when she left Madame Vood's place. As she made her way to her car, she couldn't prevent her eyes from darting around in search of Midnight and men in cloaks. She had to remind herself that she didn't believe in talking spirits or angels or whatever Madame Vood wanted to call them.

She was so preoccupied she didn't even see the woman from Jessie's Diner walking up the driveway until she'd almost plowed into her.

"Oh." The woman stopped short. "You were our waitress last night."

"Kat," Kat said with a nod. "You're Monica, right?"

"You have a good memory." Monica

grinned. "And that pumpkin ravioli was delicious. You can tell Jessie I said so."

"I will."

Monica's gaze strayed past Kat's shoulder. "Were you just with Madame Vood?"

Kat hesitated, not wanting to admit to having sought out the services of a ghost whisperer. "You know her?" she said instead.

Monica shrugged, looking as reluctant as Kat to admit to anything. "I've been here a few times. This is about my fourth visit."

"Yeah?" Kat was surprised someone had found Madame Vood's insights noteworthy enough to return for a repeat session.

"Truth be told, my mother's dementia has taken a hard toll on my family," Monica said. "She's deteriorated a lot in the past year. My father died a decade ago, but she's started talking about him again as if he's still around."

Kat saw tears welling in Monica's eyes, and her heart went out to her. "That has to be tough."

"It is." Monica twined her fingers together. "I thought I'd come to terms with Dad's death, but now that Mom keeps dredging up old memories I'm starting to realize maybe I'm not as healed as I thought I was."

"And talking to a fortune teller helps you?" Kat asked.

"She's a spiritual guidance counselor."

"Right."

"And yes, she helps me. Some of the things she says . . ." Monica bit her lip. "It's like Dad is right there in the room with us."

Kat nodded. An hour ago she would have dismissed Monica as a woman so desperate to connect with her late father that she would believe anything, but after her own session she had to admit Madame Vood was good. She'd even had Kat going for a minute.

Monica sighed, wrapping her arms around her middle. "When Mom starts talking about Dad, it's like ripping old wounds open. Not only does it feel like I'm losing him all over again, but her rambling emphasizes how we're losing her too."

"I'm sorry," Kat said, unable to think of a more comforting response.

"This whole thing has been especially hard on Beth. She and Mom used to be so close. I've tried to get her to come to a session with Madame Vood, but she refuses. She tells me she has no interest in talking to the dead, that she'd rather focus on getting her grandma back to normal." Monica's eyes filled with tears. "Like dementia is a curable disease."

Monica's misery was contagious. Kat felt a lump forming in her own throat.

Monica fumbled in her purse, pulling out a tissue. "Oh, look at me. I can't even talk about Mom without falling apart."

"It's okay," Kat said.

Monica blew her nose and wiped her cheeks. "Tell me, have you found that missing cat yet?"

Kat shook her head. "We had search parties looking for him all evening with no luck."

"That's too bad." Monica offered Kat a watery smile. "I looked for him a little after leaving Jessie's, you know. My friend Heather called and asked if I would help. I tried to get Beth to come too. I thought it would give us some time to bond."

"But she didn't want to go?" Kat guessed.

Monica's face fell. "She said she had a date, but later I heard her on the phone asking Luke to come pick her up. I think she made up the date story to avoid spending time with me."

"Is Luke kind of tall and lanky?" Kat asked, holding her hand above her head at Lindsay's brother's approximate height.

"Yes," Monica said. "Luke Mackinaw. Do

you know him?"

"I met him yesterday, at the copy shop. His sister works there."

Monica smiled. "Lindsay is a good girl. She reminds me of my Beth."

Kat studied her. "But you don't like Luke."

Monica's smile dimmed. "It's not that I don't like him. I would just prefer that he not date my daughter."

"Why's that?"

"He doesn't strike me as very ambitious. Beth is an excellent student, near straight As. Luke, on the other hand, can barely be bothered to pass his classes."

"And you're worried his study habits will rub off on her?" Kat surmised.

Monica nodded. "She's a senior. The last thing she needs is to lose interest in school now, when she has less than a year left before she graduates. She's applying early admission to University of Washington, but even if she's accepted I told her it's important to maintain a good GPA all the way through June."

"Has she given you any reason to worry?"

"No, not really." Monica stuffed the tissue back in her purse. "But Beth is so vulnerable right now, with Mom in the nursing home. I fear the stress will get to her and her grades will start slipping."

Kat's mouth curved up. She found it rather touching how concerned Monica seemed to be about Beth's future. She wondered if her own mother had worried that much about her. If she had, she had only done so from afar, while Kat was tied up in the Cherry Hills foster care system.

Kat cleared her throat before she could get too caught up in her own memories. "I should get going. I'm sure you're anxious to talk to Madame Vood."

Monica didn't appear to hear her. "Hear that?" she asked, tilting her head to one side.

Kat listened for a moment, but she could only detect the faint chirping of faraway birds and a car driving past in the distance. "Hear what?"

Monica's face had paled. "It sounds like a ghost."

"I don't hear anything." For that matter, Kat wasn't even sure what she was listening for. What did ghosts sound like?

"This isn't the first time I've heard a ghost here." Monica's eyes veered toward Madame Vood's house before landing back on Kat. "I bet she has spirits all around her property, clamoring to talk to the loved ones they were forced to leave behind."

Kat glanced around, the hairs on the back of her neck standing up. It took her a second before she remembered she didn't believe in ghosts.

"The old Lerner place is not too far from here either," Monica continued, gesturing toward her left. "I'm positive that place is haunted."

"The Lerners?" The name sounded familiar, but Kat couldn't place it.

"They moved to Cherry Hills after they married, about twenty years ago. He was in a wheelchair."

"Oh, right." Kat remembered them now. She'd even run into the Lerners once or twice when she was a teenager.

"They had been trying to conceive for forever and only succeeded about two years ago." Monica pursed her lips. "Unfortunately, there were complications when it came time for her to give birth. She died, and so did the baby."

A stone settled in Kat's stomach. "That's terrible."

"Yes. And the husband didn't last but three

days later. He dropped dead of a heart attack right in the middle of their living room." Monica sighed. "It's like their love was the only thing keeping him tethered to this world."

Kat considered that, recalling what Madame Vood had told her about ghosts. "If the whole family died, what makes you think their place is haunted? I thought ghosts only hung around if they had unfinished business to attend to."

Monica pulled her purse closer. "I can't explain it. But I'm not the only one who believes it. While we were out last night my friend Heather heard the baby's spirit knocking around the Lerner house. Their property was never sold, you know."

Kat cinched her jacket tighter, trying to muster up some warmth. Her bones had gone cold.

Monica coughed. "But anyway, if the Lerners do have unfinished business here on Earth, I don't suppose it's within my power to help them. I don't have the type of talent that Madame Vood does."

Kat looked at the sign advertising Madame Vood's business hours. "Right."

"Well, I should let you go." Monica took a step up the driveway. "It was nice chatting with you."

"You too."

Kat watched Monica approach Madame Vood's front door. She hoped Monica's visit ended on a more satisfying note than hers had.

CHAPTER EIGHT

Kat's cell phone rang while she was walking into her apartment unit. She pulled it out of her pocket, her spirits soaring when she saw Willow's name displayed on the caller ID.

"Tell me you found Midnight," Kat answered in lieu of a greeting.

"Sorry," Willow said.

Kat closed her apartment door and sagged against it. "It's okay. I just feel like we're running out of time. Today is Halloween, and we're no closer to finding him than we were yesterday."

"That's why I called. I was hoping we could look for him together, if you're free."

"Sure. Where do you want to meet?"

"I'll pick you up at your apartment," Willow said. "I want to take some of your fliers with us."

"Okay. See you soon."

Tom padded down the hallway, twining between Kat's legs as he welcomed her back home.

She reached down to scratch his head. "I missed you too, baby. You want to go outside with us today?"

Tom rubbed the side of his face against Kat's shoe and meowed.

"I don't know if that's a yes or a no," Kat replied. But she figured there was an easy way to find out.

She stepped into the living room and plucked Tom's harness and leash off of the coffee table. When Tom saw what she was holding, his eyes grew wide and he bolted back down the hallway, presumably to hide under the bed.

Kat snorted. "I guess that answers my question."

Matty lifted her head up from where she had been napping on the couch. Spying the leash dangling from Kat's fingers, the feline jumped up and rocketed toward the front door as if the apartment were on fire.

Kat had to shake her head at how different the two animals were. "We have to wait for Willow," she told the tortoiseshell.

Matty wasn't interested in excuses. She looked pointedly at the door and meowed.

When Willow buzzed to be let into the building, Matty was still hovering by the door. She had moved on from staring at it to taking decisive action, alternating between trying to wedge her paw through the crack at the bottom and reaching for the doorknob.

Kat had to pick Matty up to let Willow inside. "She's anxious to start searching."

Willow smiled and gave Matty a light pat on the head. "That's sweet."

"She would have stayed out all last night if I didn't finally make her come home."

Willow's smile faded. "This is all my fault. After everything I've put her through, I wouldn't be surprised if Tracy no longer talks to me in the teachers' lounge."

"I'm sure she doesn't blame you," Kat told her.

Willow's shoulders sagged. "How can she not? He was my responsibility."

Kat didn't reply. It was obvious nothing she

could say would ease Willow's sense of guilt.

"What do you know about Tracy's neighbor, Connie Vood?" Kat asked, deciding a subject change might keep Willow from brooding.

"I've never talked to her." Willow rubbed her nose. "In truth, I kind of went out of my way to avoid her. Witches give me the willies."

"She's a spiritual guidance counselor."

"Whatever you want to call her, according to Tracy she has an in with the dead. I'd rather not get on her radar if that's true. She might send my ancestors to spy on me or something."

Matty had started squirming, so Kat set her on the floor. "I met with her this morning. She said Midnight is close."

Willow angled her head to one side. "What does that mean?"

"I have no idea. Supposedly an angel gave her the information, but they don't measure distance like we do." Kat smacked her palm against her forehead. "Listen to me, talking about otherworldly beings like they actually know where Midnight is. I'm letting this whole Halloween thing get to me."

Willow released a small laugh. "It's impossible not to get in the spirit when everybody else is. Halloween is all my students have been talking about this week."

"I actually ran into a few of your students yesterday," Kat said.

"Yeah?" Willow regarded her. "Which ones?"

"Lindsay. She works down at the copy shop. Although, I'm not sure if she's in any of your classes. I just know she goes to Cherry Hills High."

"Lindsay Mackinaw," Willow confirmed with a nod. "Good student. She doesn't have a natural aptitude for the language arts, but she studies hard."

"I met her brother Luke and his girlfriend Beth too," Kat told Willow.

"Ah, Beth." Willow sighed. "She used to be one of these students who couldn't wait to be engaged. She raised her hand in class and got excited when she aced a test. Now, she's still keeping her grades up and turning in her homework, but you can tell her heart's not really in it anymore."

Kat played through her conversation with Monica. "Maybe once things settle down with her grandmother she'll get some of her spark back."

"I hope so." Willow surveyed Kat's apartment. "So, you have more fliers here?"

"They're on the coffee table."

Kat walked into the living room, frowning when she saw Matty sitting on top of the fliers. She tried to nudge the cat aside, but Matty went limp, tipping over like a dropped paperweight.

Willow laughed. "She's determined to make you work for what you want."

Kat prodded the feline with her fingertips. "Come on, Matty. Let me give these to Willow, and then we'll all go outside."

Instead of obliging, Matty stretched her front paws out as far as she could. Her toes brushed against something, prompting her to lift her head. Her eyes glinted with mischief when she spotted the piece of paper just out of reach. She scrambled upright, her hind feet kicking at the stack of fliers and scattering them everywhere.

"Matty!" Kat snatched a handful of fliers off the floor. "Look at the mess you made."

Matty responded by batting the scrap of paper around until it too fell onto the floor.

The commotion drew Tom out of the bedroom. When he saw the papers spread across the carpet he dashed over and lay down on top of them. His tail swept back and forth, his eyes slipping closed in his contentment.

"Tom!" Kat scolded.

"Let me help," Willow said.

Willow stepped around Kat and picked up Matty's makeshift toy. She was about to put it back on the coffee table when her hand stilled. "This is the code to get into Tracy's house," she said.

"I know. Matty found it in Connie Vood's yard last night."

Willow held the paper up to her face. "Connie Vood didn't write this."

"I'm guessing whoever broke into Tracy's house dropped it when they were fleeing the scene." Kat frowned, the implication of Willow's statement sinking in. "But how do *you* know it didn't come from Connie Vood?"

"Because I recognize this handwriting." Willow's knuckles had turned white from her hold on the paper. "Luke Mackinaw wrote this."

CHAPTER NINE

Kat was nearly breathless by the time she burst into the copy shop. Although she'd taken her car, the short drive hadn't given her enough time to recuperate from her sprint through her apartment building.

Lindsay looked up from the computer when the door chime announced Kat's entrance. "Hi again. You need more fliers printed?"

"No." Kat gulped air into her lungs as she hurried over to the counter. "Where's Luke?"

Lindsay's forehead furrowed. "My brother?"

"Is he here?" Kat's eyes roved around the store as if she might spot him hunched behind one of the copy machines. "I need to talk to him about Midnight."

"Midnight?" Lindsay blinked. "You mean the cat on your fliers? The one that belongs to Ms. Montgomery?"

Kat nodded. "I know he took her. I know he was the one who broke into Tracy's house."

Lindsay's mouth dropped open. "Are you sure?"

"I found a piece of paper with Tracy's door code written on it. Willow Wu recognized Luke's handwriting. She's graded enough of his papers to know how he writes."

"But how would Luke know Ms. Montgomery's door code?"

"I don't know, but he got it from somewhere."

"Wait a minute." Lindsay straightened, blowing a strand of her honey-blond hair away from her face. "Luke couldn't have taken Midnight. There's nowhere to hide him in the house without me or my parents seeing."

Kat flattened her palms on the counter. "If you're covering for him, I'll find out. Willow is on her way over to your house right now in case Luke is there."

Lindsay spread her hands. "I'm not lying."

The bell on the door sounded. Kat's heart lurched when Luke strolled into the store.

"You're not off yet?" he asked Lindsay. "You told me you only work until eleven on Saturdays."

"Luke," Lindsay said, coming around to their side of the counter. Her eyes were hard as they zeroed in on her brother. "Did you break into Ms. Montgomery's house?"

Luke froze in his tracks. "Uh, wh—what are you talking about?"

Lindsay stood on her tiptoes and jabbed a finger against his chest. "Did you do it?"

Luke's gaze skirted toward the large glass windows lining the front of the store. He looked like a caged animal planning to make a run for it.

"Oh, Luke." Lindsay stomped her foot on the floor, her hand falling back to her side. "I can't believe you would be that stupid. How did you even get Ms. Montgomery's door code?"

Luke flushed. "Before she left, I overheard her giving Ms. Wu the combination. They were standing right there in the school hallway."

Lindsay stared at him, shaking her head like a disappointed mother. It took Kat a second to remember that Luke was actually the older of the two.

Luke shoved his hands in his jeans pockets.

"Look, I just wanted to change a couple test scores, okay? Just a few Ds to Bs."

Lindsay's blue eyes flashed. "Did you really think you'd get away with it? That Ms. Montgomery wouldn't remember giving you Ds?"

Luke toed the carpet with one sneaker, not saying anything as he stared at his feet.

Lindsay's eyes met Kat's, and she grimaced. "You were right."

Kat approached Luke, imploring him with her eyes. "Wherever you're holding Midnight, you have to give him back."

Luke rocked backward, her statement seeming to knock him off-balance. "I don't have Midnight."

Kat's hands clenched into fists. "Don't lie. Whatever your problem is with Tracy, don't take it out on an innocent animal."

"I don't have him, I swear."

"I'm not interested in punishing you," Kat said. "Tracy just wants you to return him safely."

"I already told you, I don't have him," Luke insisted. "Yes, I went into her house, but I didn't take the cat."

Kat paused. Something in Luke's tone made

her believe him. "Are you saying Midnight wasn't there when you broke in?"

"The cat was there. But I didn't take him."

"Midnight snuck out the door when you left then." Despite Tracy's claim that Midnight would have never ventured outside voluntarily, Kat certainly preferred that to someone snatching him for evil purposes.

Luke shook his head. "We would have seen him if he'd followed us."

Kat's breath hitched. "We? What do you mean 'we would have seen him'? Somebody else was with you?"

"No!" He eyed the glass storefront again, his face turning beet red. "I meant me. I was there alone. I'm being totally truthful."

Lindsay heaved a sigh. "Oh, Luke. What did you do?"

He whipped toward her. "Nothing. I just changed a few grades. That's all."

"Who was there with you?" Kat asked.

"Nobody." He blew out a breath. "I told you already. I was there—alone—to alter a few test scores. No big deal. I just wanted to boost my GPA a little, so maybe I can get into U-Dub."

"U-Dub?" Goosebumps broke out on Kat's skin as she replayed her conversation with

Monica, the truth hitting her like a sledge-hammer. "Beth was the person with you."

Luke's mouth twitched. "No," he said, but he hesitated too long for Kat to believe him.

"Luke, please don't lie." Kat had to tamp down her urge to yell, guessing that would only encourage him to clam up. "I know you and Beth are a couple, and I know she's applying for early admission to University of Washington. I'm guessing she plans to go with or without you."

Pain rippled across Luke's face, and Kat knew she had pegged the situation correctly. But she failed to derive any satisfaction from being right. Luke had to be devastated by the knowledge that life was taking him and the person he loved in two different directions.

Kat looked him in the eye. "I have a question for you, and I need an honest answer. Was Beth inside Tracy's house with you?"

Luke shifted his feet. "Okay, so maybe she was there."

Lindsay set her hands on her hips and shook her head.

Luke straightened. "But Beth didn't do any-thing. I was the one who punched in the lock code and changed those grades. She just stood there the whole time. And we didn't take Ms. Montgomery's cat."

"I believe you," Kat said.

She meant it. Not only did Luke look sincere, but he didn't strike her as the type to take someone's pet for nefarious reasons. He was simply a boy willing to do anything he could to improve his chances of staying with the girl he loved.

The only problem was, Kat's conviction in his innocence meant she still didn't know who had taken Midnight.

But she did have one guess.

CHAPTER TEN

Monica looked startled to see Kat standing on her doorstep. "Oh, it's you," she said. "Hi."

Kat mustered up a smile. "Sorry to barge over like this, but I really need to talk to Beth. Do you know where I can find her?"

"She's in her bedroom." Monica's eyes narrowed. "But what kind of business do you have with Beth?"

"I have a question for her."

Monica regarded her. Kat considered explaining, but she didn't want to accuse Beth without giving her a chance to tell her side of the story first.

"What's going on?"

Monica swiveled around. Beth stood at the base of the staircase, a puzzled look on her face.

"Are you guys talking about me?" she asked. "I heard my name."

Monica swung the front door wide and motioned Kat inside. "Kat's here to see you, honey."

Kat hurried over the threshold before Monica could change her mind about letting her in. "I wanted to ask you something," she said to Beth.

Monica shut the door and folded her hands in front of her. The three of them stood there, exchanging awkward glances. Kat had hoped Monica would excuse herself, but it soon became clear that wasn't going to happen.

"Do you mind if I speak to Beth in private?" Kat asked.

Monica started to shake her head.

"It's okay, Mom," Beth piped up. "I'll yell if I need you."

Monica stood there for another second. Then she shrugged and took a step toward the staircase. She ascended slowly, as though to give Beth plenty of time to change her mind.

As soon as Monica disappeared out of sight,

Kat faced Beth. "You took Midnight."

Beth didn't look surprised by the accusation. She had probably already deduced that her involvement in Midnight's catnapping was the only reason Kat would have to show up looking for her.

"I didn't mean to make Ms. Montgomery worry," Beth said, perching on the couch arm-rest behind her. "Luke—" She abruptly stopped talking, a flush creeping up her neck.

"I know you and Luke were there to change his grades," Kat said. "He admitted it."

Beth set her jaw. "He told on me?"

"He didn't mention you. I figured that part out myself."

Beth chewed on one fingernail, appearing to take that in.

Kat looked around the living room. "Where's Midnight?"

Beth's hand fell away from her mouth. "He's not here. My dad's allergic."

Panic bubbled up Kat's chest. If Midnight wasn't here—

"He's okay," Beth hastened to add before Kat had time to imagine the worst. "He has food and water."

Indignation rose inside Kat's chest. "Food

and water isn't everything a pet needs to thrive. They need love and companionship too."

"Oh, I didn't take him to keep him." Beth looked shocked that Kat had come to such a conclusion. "I was just borrowing him for the weekend."

Kat's stomach tightened. "Borrowing him to do what?"

"To show my grandma." Beth's face fell. "She can't have pets where she's at. Since Ms. Montgomery was going to be out of town, I thought if I just took him for a couple days I could return him before she got home. I didn't know she'd freak out and fly back early."

Kat absorbed that. If she had to guess, she'd bet Beth hadn't considered the consequences of her actions beyond how she and her grandmother might benefit. She'd probably taken one look at Midnight and formulated a plan right then and there, never asking herself what Willow Wu would do when she walked into Tracy's house the next morning.

"Nana's mind is going," Beth said, averting her eyes. "She rarely knows who I am anymore. But she loves Halloween. At least, she used to. So I thought maybe if I surrounded her with enough Halloween stuff, she'd come back for a little while. I mean, if I can get her to remember how much fun we used to have together carving jack-o'-lanterns and going trick-or-treating, she has to remember how we're related, don't you think?"

Kat's heart wrenched as Beth's face crumpled. It was clear the girl missed her grandmother—at least the grandmother who knew who she was—terribly.

Beth drew in a shaky breath, wiping her tears away with one hand. "Anyway, I've been planning this thing for her this weekend. I bought some pumpkins and costumes and stuff. Later today Luke and I are going to drive up to Nana's and surprise her." Beth paused, then said, "Midnight was kinda a last-minute addition. Luke doesn't even know about him yet. When we were in Ms. Montgomery's house he was so friendly that I thought . . ."

"You thought he would make a great Halloween accessory," Kat filled in.

Beth nodded. "Luke had Ms. Montgomery's door code jotted down on a slip of paper. After he threw it away, I grabbed it out of the garbage when he wasn't looking. Then I snuck out of here and walked back to Ms. Montgomery's house later that night to borrow him."

"Where are you keeping him?" Kat asked.

"In the old Lerner house."

Kat recalled what Monica had said about the abandoned house being haunted. Could all the eerie cries and weird noises Monica and her friend had heard in the past twenty-four hours have originated not from discontented spirits but from a scared cat who just wanted to go home?

The thought made Kat's stomach twist.

"I would have waited until today to take him, but I couldn't break in on a Saturday afternoon," Beth said.

Kat pivoted around and strode toward the door. "We have to go get him. Now."

After making sure Beth was following her, Kat ran to her car. She couldn't move fast enough as she unlocked the doors and threw herself into the driver's seat.

Beth moved more slowly, opening the passenger door and climbing inside with all the speed of a slug. But Kat didn't complain. She was just glad Beth was getting into the car.

When Beth was finally situated, Kat tossed her her cell phone. "Call Tracy and tell her what you did," she ordered. "Tell her to meet us at the Lerner house. Her number's on that flier on the floorboard."

Beth didn't move. The thought of confessing everything to her teacher seemed to have immobilized her.

"Do it," Kat commanded, shoving the car into gear.

Beth must have realized she meant business. She jerked upright and fumbled with the phone.

Kat only half listened to Beth's end of the conversation as she sped toward Tracy's neighborhood. She was vaguely aware of the teenager explaining her motive for taking the cat, but she had too much adrenaline running through her arteries to stay focused on Beth's words.

Kat had just turned off the main road when Beth lowered the phone to her lap. "Tell me how to get to the Lerner house," Kat said.

Beth aimed a trembling finger out the windshield. "Take a right up there. It's the house with the unmowed lawn."

Kat did as instructed, suppressing her desire to stomp on the accelerator.

The house was easy to recognize. As the only one on this block falling into disrepair, it stood out from the well-maintained homes surrounding it.

Kat pulled into the driveway and shoved the car into park. She took her cell phone back from Beth, and they both got out of the car.

"You lead the way," Kat said.

Beth pointed toward the side of the house. "There's a broken window over here."

They had to take exaggerated steps in order to wade through the overgrowth. When they reached the back of the house, Kat saw the window Beth had mentioned.

She also heard the most heartbreaking mewl to ever reach her ears.

Kat picked up her pace. "Stay out here and wait for Tracy. I'm going to get Midnight."

Beth stopped walking. "Okay."

Kat crawled gingerly through the window, careful not to cut herself on the jagged shards of glass protruding from the frame. It was harder than she thought to maintain her balance without touching the sides of the window.

Somehow, she made it inside without any injuries. Glass crunched beneath her shoes, and she reached for the wall to steady herself. She tried not to cringe as her hand touched what felt like a spiderweb, Beth's motives for choosing this place becoming clearer. Nobody in their right mind would enter this house unless they had to.

"Midnight?" she called out. "Where are you, baby?"

Her heart rate skyrocketed when she heard a meow.

Kat followed Midnight's cries to a closed door. As anxious as she was to free him, she forced herself to move slowly so as not to startle or hit the cat if he happened to be sitting right behind the door.

Dust filled her nostrils as she let herself into the room. Although a handful of boards had been hammered over the windows, enough sunlight seeped through the gaps to illuminate scores of minuscule particles dancing in the air. Kat had no choice but to sneeze.

Something brushed against her foot. When she looked down to see Midnight weaving between her legs, she felt fifty pounds lighter.

She bent down and scooped up the cat. He let her, seeming happy to have the company. She buried her face in his fur, a surge of emotion ripping through her. The tension that had been building inside of her ever since she'd learned about Midnight's disappearance drained from her body in that one instant, releasing with it a steady stream of tears.

"Midnight?" she heard Tracy call out.

Midnight must have recognized his human's voice. His ears pricked, and he meowed.

Kat let out one last sob before swallowing the lump in her throat. "In here!"

Tracy came barreling into the room. Midnight started squirming at the sight of her, his meows coming faster now.

"Midnight!" Tracy squealed, rushing toward him.

Kat handed him over. "He's okay."

Tracy hugged him close to her chest, her own tears pouring out.

Kat turned away to give them some privacy, wiping the moisture from her cheeks. Her gaze caught on Beth standing just outside the room, and a mixture of anger and resentment seared through her. Now that she knew Midnight was safe, her relief was clearing the way for a whole host of other emotions.

Kat twisted toward Tracy. "Would you like me to call the police? They can figure out how to deal with Beth."

Beth shifted her weight between her feet. From the terrified look in her eyes, Kat figured this was the first time the teenager had ever been on the wrong side of the law.

Tracy continued to stroke Midnight while she blinked her tears away. "I don't know. Maybe we could leave them out of this."

Kat arched an eyebrow. "Leave them out of this? She broke into your house and stole your cat."

"I know, but you heard her reasons." Tracy shifted her attention to Beth. "You still fixing to go to your nana's tonight?"

Beth shrugged. "I guess." She glanced at Kat before looking down at her shoes. "I mean, if I'm not in jail."

Tracy adjusted Midnight in her arms. "Why don't I go on up to Wenatchee with you?"

Beth's head snapped up. "What do you mean?"

"If you're game, I can tote Midnight up to your nana's like you wanted," Tracy said. "I'm not doing anything tonight. I hadn't even planned to be back in town until tomorrow. It wouldn't hurt me to take a drive with y'all."

Beth gaped at her. "You would do that?"

"Sure." Tracy gave Midnight a kiss. "Like you said, if anything can make your nana remember who she is, Midnight's your best bet. And if he can't do the trick, well, then I reckon he can at least provide her with a couple hours of joy."

Finally, it was Beth's turn to cry.

CHAPTER ELEVEN

Andrew shut the front door and walked back into the living room. "That must have been trick-or-treater number five thousand six hundred and twelve."

Kat smirked. "Try seventeen."

Andrew slumped next to her on the couch. "Really? That's it?"

"Want me to get the next batch?"

"That only seems fair, since you were the one who talked me into this."

Kat grinned. "For all your grousing, you look awfully happy. You have this glow about you."

"That's sweat." He sagged against the sofa. "I'm exhausted."

Kat laughed, her gaze drifting toward Matty, who had located a space behind a video game console on one of Andrew's entertainment shelves. The feline was lazing contentedly in her new spot, keeping one eye on the humans.

Tom, on the other hand, hadn't sat still since they'd arrived. At the moment he was inspecting every box, bag, and appliance in Andrew's kitchen. Knowing how he liked table scraps, Kat had to wonder if he was searching for something to eat besides the bowl of kibble she had brought with them.

She hadn't planned to take Matty and Tom with her to Andrew's, but as she was leaving her apartment she had been seized by a memory of Midnight crying for help. She had known then she couldn't go anywhere without her own fur babies by her side. Thinking about Midnight's ordeal still caused a physical ache deep in her chest.

Kat fingered her hair, wondering how the visit with Beth's grandmother was going. No sooner had the thought entered her mind when the image of an elderly woman flashed through her head. The woman had her head thrown back in laughter, her white hair framing her face as she rested two liver-spotted hands on the pure-black cat in her lap. A freshly carved pumpkin sat on the table next to her, a smile etched beneath two triangular eyes.

Kat blinked, and the image disappeared. She frowned, wondering if she'd just had what Madame Vood might call a vision. Was there any chance that the white-haired woman was Beth's grandmother?

No, Kat thought. *That would be crazy.*

"Your cats like it here," Andrew piped up, drawing Kat from her thoughts.

She looked at him, her heart skipping a beat when her eyes met his. "I like it here too."

Andrew brushed a lock of hair away from her face. "I could get used to having you here."

"I could get used to being here."

Andrew leaned close enough for his breath to warm Kat's skin. Her pulse quickened, and she ran her tongue over her lips. The way he was looking at her, she knew he was getting ready to kiss her.

Except, he didn't. Right before his lips touched hers, he pulled back, a muscle in his jaw clenching. As clearly as if she could read his mind, she knew he was thinking about his uncle's fate and all those old girlfriends who had only lasted long enough to see the inside of his house once.

"Andrew," she said, "I realize you have a superstition about people in—"

He pressed one finger to her lips, cutting her off. "Don't say it. I don't want to jinx this."

The doorbell rang. Kat didn't move, hoping whoever was there would go away.

Andrew draped his arms across the back of the couch. "Your turn to get that, remember?"

His flat tone sent a chill down her spine. She hated to leave him before they could talk about what had just happened, but when the doorbell rang again she realized she didn't have a choice.

She hauled herself off the couch with a sigh. Her mind was still on Andrew as she swung the door open, but when she caught sight of the person on the doorstep she forgot all about their interrupted conversation.

Standing in front of her was a short man in a cloak. His face was covered by a plastic mask that featured one bulging eye, several bloody scars, and a crooked nose.

Kat gaped at him, Madame Vood's words from this morning echoing through her head. *The spirit tells me he will send you a sign when you are safe to inhabit this new world.*

This couldn't be the sign the spirit had been

talking about, could it?

"Trick or treat," the short man said, holding out a pillowcase.

His squeaky voice caused Kat to relax a little. Okay, so this wasn't a man after all, but a boy dressed as . . . Well, she couldn't really tell what he was supposed to be, but with the mask and cloak she was guessing something evil.

The pillowcase drooped. "Do you have any candy?" the boy asked.

"Oh." Kat shook herself and hurried to grab a few pieces of candy from the bowl on the table next to the door. "Yes, sorry." She dropped them into his pillowcase.

"Thanks, lady."

Before Kat could reply, the boy whirled around and raced across the yard to the next house.

Kat watched him for a second, feeling disoriented. What had just happened?

She shut the door and hobbled back to the couch.

Andrew sat up. "What's wrong? You look like you just saw a ghost."

Kat met his gaze, a smile breaking out on her face. The chill she had felt earlier was gone now, replaced by a warmth spreading throughout every cell in her body.

"I don't know if he was a ghost, a spirit, or just a boy in a costume," she said, perching next to Andrew, "but I think he just gave us his blessing."

NOTE FROM THE AUTHOR

Thank you for visiting Cherry Hills, home of Kat, Matty, and Tom! If you enjoyed their story, please consider leaving a book review on your favorite retailer and/or review site.

Keep reading for an excerpt from Book Eight of the Cozy Cat Caper Mystery series, *Stabbed in Cherry Hills*, and descriptions of some of the other books in the series. Thank you!

Excerpt From

STABBED
in CHERRY
HILLS

COZY CAT

A CAPER

MYSTERY
BOOK

8

PAIGE SLEUTH

So, how did it go?" Andrew Milhone asked as he stepped inside Katherine Harper's apartment.

Kat kicked the door shut. "Awful. It was the worst job interview in recorded history."

Tom, Kat's brown-and-black cat, poked his head out of the kitchen. When he spotted Andrew, his ears pricked and he ran over to them, meowing the whole way.

"What do you think, Tommy boy?" Andrew asked, crouching down. "You think your mommy's interview was as bad as she's making it out to be?"

Tom responded by flopping onto one side and splaying his legs.

Andrew lifted one eyebrow. "Wow. That must have been one dire interview."

"I told you." Kat trudged into the living room and slumped onto the couch. "My chances of getting the job would have been better if I hadn't even shown up today."

Andrew stood up and took off his coat. "Yeah, but then you'd have to wait until your first day on the job to humiliate yourself."

Kat stuck her tongue out at him.

Andrew's eyes twinkled as he walked toward her. But he didn't get very far before Tom scrambled upright and raced in front of him, coming to a halt in the exact spot where Andrew was about to step.

Andrew pulled his foot back at the last second, narrowly avoiding stepping on Tom's tail. But the abrupt motion caused him to lose his balance. He pitched forward, his coat flying out of his hands. He somehow managed to catch himself on the sofa armrest, ending up only half sprawled on the floor.

Kat's heart lurched, and she bent closer to him. "Are you all right?"

He blew his sandy hair out of his eyes. "Your cat almost killed me."

"Next time don't be the first to walk away,"

Kat advised, relaxing a little now that she knew he wasn't injured. "As long as he's still lingering, he hasn't gotten enough attention yet."

Andrew got back on his feet. "I didn't think he ever got enough."

Kat grinned. "It's a very rare occurrence."

Andrew circled around to the front of the couch. Tom watched his progress with the intensity of a hawk. His dilated pupils suggested he was contemplating the merits of attempting another dash-and-stop. He looked almost disappointed when Andrew plopped onto the seat next to Kat, eliminating the feline's chances of tripping him again.

"So, give me all the details about this interview," Andrew said, draping his arm around Kat's shoulders.

She sagged against him. "You sure you want to know?"

"Whatever happened, I doubt it was as bad as you're making it out to be."

"Really? My interviewer's name was Leo Price, but I was so nervous I botched it and called him Mr. Lice."

Andrew chuckled.

"It's not funny," she said.

"It's a little funny."

She considered arguing with him, then opted to let it go. "Well, what happened next isn't funny. When I reached out to shake his hand, I knocked over his coffee mug and spilled hot coffee all over the front of his pants."

"It was an accident. Anybody could have done the same."

"Have you ever poured coffee on Chief Kenny's lap?" she challenged.

"Well, no."

"And that wasn't even the worst part of the interview." Kat's stomach clenched just thinking about what had occurred next. "After he dried himself off as best he could, he asked about my prior programming experience."

"So?"

"So that's when I told him about that database project I worked on in college as part of Professor Bluefield's team."

Andrew tilted his head. "You mean the one to track the trees planted on your campus? Didn't you say your department gave you some kind of award for that database?"

"I did."

"So what's the problem?"

"The problem is, as it turns out, Leo and my old professor went to high school together thirty years ago. At the end of their senior year, Professor Bluefield stole Leo's girlfriend away and married her himself."

Andrew winced. "Ouch."

Kat sighed. "Exactly. I wish I had known that before I listed Professor Bluefield as a reference."

"Leo might not have even seen that. If DataRightly operates anything like the Cherry Hills Police Department, their Human Resources department handles all the reference checks."

Kat rested the back of her head against Andrew's arm and stared up at the ceiling. "The way my luck is going, I doubt it."

As if sensing her need for comfort, Matty, Kat's yellow-and-brown tortoiseshell cat, jumped onto the cushion next to her and settled down against her leg. Kat rested her palm on Matty's back. The feel of the feline's soft, warm body underneath her fingers did wonders to lift some of her dejection.

So as not to be left out, Tom leapt onto Andrew's lap. He tilted his head to one side as if to question why Andrew had stopped with the belly rubs. Andrew responded by scratching Tom between the ears. Apparently that was an acceptable answer. Tom started kneading Andrew's leg with his front paws, his claws extending and contracting as the sound of his purring filled the air.

Kat rolled her head sideways until Andrew was in her direct line of vision. "I'm worried I'll never find a job in my field unless I move to Seattle or someplace with more tech companies. There just aren't a lot of options in Central Washington."

She felt Andrew's arm tense under her head. "Are you thinking of moving?" he asked.

"I'd prefer not to. I like it here."

Andrew scooted closer to her. "I'm glad. I like having you back in Cherry Hills."

She snuggled against him, marveling at how her perspective had changed since she'd moved back to her childhood hometown four months ago. Back in July she hadn't felt much of an attachment to Cherry Hills. Now, she couldn't imagine being happy anywhere else.

"I just wish more local places were looking for programmers," she said, brushing a wad of loose fur off of Matty and watching it drift toward the carpet. "At this rate, I'll be waitressing at Jessie's Diner until I qualify for social security."

The sound of Andrew's cell ringtone interrupted their conversation. He eased his arm away from Kat and fished the phone out of his pants pocket, careful not to disturb Tom as he did so. "Milhone," he answered.

Kat watched him as she stroked Matty, a little buzz of energy zipping through her body. Sometimes she still couldn't believe they were a couple. When they were growing up together, she never would have imagined that one day their relationship would morph into something romantic.

"I'll be right there," Andrew said before pulling his phone away from his ear and disconnecting the call.

His grim tone prompted Kat to sit up straighter. "What's wrong?"

Andrew nudged Tom aside and stood up. "I have to go."

Kat scrambled off the couch, ignoring the dirty look Matty shot her. "But you just got off work. I thought we were going to eat dinner together."

"Well, apparently I was only on a short break."

Kat had trouble breathing as she watched him shove his phone back into his pocket and scoop his coat off of the floor. As a police detective, there were only a few reasons why Andrew might be called back to work. None of them were pleasant.

He stopped walking halfway to the front door and turned around. The light she had seen in his eyes earlier was gone now. "Kat, you're going to hear this sooner or later, so I might as well be the one to tell you," he said.

Her heart stopped beating. "What's that?"

"Leo Price was just found stabbed outside the DataRightly building." Andrew's jaw clenched. "He didn't make it, Kat. He's dead."

* * *

Please check your favorite online retailer for availability.

THANKSGIVING
in CHERRY
HILLS

Thanksgiving is a time for crime in Cherry Hills, Washington.

Kat Harper expects her biggest Thanksgiving challenge to be coming up with an edible vegan pumpkin pie, but that all changes when a woman is mugged outside her apartment building. Unfortunately, Sylvia Garcia isn't the only victim of this cruel act. Sylvia had only just finished food shopping on behalf of a local homeless shelter before she was attacked, and the thief made off with all her spoils. Now it's questionable whether the less fortunate residents of Cherry Hills will have much to be thankful for this holiday season.

Lucky for them, Kat's on the case. With a heaping scoop of amateur sleuthing, a pinch of determination, and a dollop of assistance from her two justice-seeking felines, Kat won't stop investigating until she's identified the guilty party. And, just maybe, she can help to put a family back together in the process.

* * *

Please check your favorite online retailer for availability.

FROZEN
in CHERRY
HILLS

First days can be killer.

Kat Harper's first day at her new job doesn't go as planned when a runaway cat leads her to a dead body outside of her office building. Things only get worse when Sadie Cramer's death is deemed a homicide, and Kat has to wonder what she's gotten herself into by accepting this position.

Much to Kat's—and her police detective boy-friend's—dismay, she soon encounters plenty of people with motive for murder. From an employee fired right before the Thanksgiving holiday, to a grown son ruthlessly cut out of an inheritance, it seems the late career counselor angered several people shortly before her passing. And now it's up to the office building's newly hired amateur sleuth to figure out exactly who is guilty . . . preferably without turning into a victim herself.

* * *

Please check your favorite online retailer for availability.

HIT & RUN
in CHERRY
HILLS

When death imitates art . . .

Cherry Hills resident Kat Harper finds herself embroiled in another murder investigation when a local artist is run down in the street. There's no question this was a deliberate act, but who was behind the wheel?

Between a money-hungry gallery owner, a brooding rival painter, and the victim's jealous sister, Kat's not sure who had more motive. And, unfortunately, nobody appears to have gotten a good look at the driver—except perhaps for an extremely territorial white cat named

Clover. But Clover is too busy guarding his favorite chair to reveal "whodunit."

That means it's up to Kat and Kat alone to track down this latest killer. Will the amateur detective succeed, or will this be the case that finally stumps her?

* * *

Please check your favorite online retailer for availability.

ABOUT THE AUTHOR

Paige Sleuth is a pseudonym for mystery author Marla Bradeen. She plots murder during the day and fights for mattress space with her two rescue cats at night. When not attending to her cats' demands, she writes. Find her at: http://www.marlabradeen.com

CPSIA information can be obtained
at www.ICGtesting.com
Printed in the USA
FSHW010545070721
83020FS

9 781533 392374